After
HAPPILY
— EVER —
AFTER

The Wicked
Stepmother
Helps Out

After Happily Ever After is published by Stone Arch Books
A Capstone Imprint
1710 Roe Crest Drive
North Mankato, Minnesota 56003
www.capstonepub.com

First published by Orchard Books, a division of Hachette Children's Books
338 Euston Road, London NW1 3BH, United Kingdom

Library of Congress Cataloging-in-Publication Data is available
on the Library of Congress website.

ISBN-13: 978-1-4342 -7951-4 (hardcover)
ISBN-13: 978-1-4342-7957-6 (paperback)

Summary: The Wicked Stepmother wants to do something to help people
and make amends for her past. But trying to find the right job proves tricky,
until the Bad Fairy gives her an idea.

Designer: Russell Griesmer
Photo Credits: ShutterStock/Maaike Boot, 4, 5, 51

Printed in China.
092013   007737LEOS14

After **HAPPILY** —EVER— **AFTER**

The Wicked
Stepmother
Helps Out

by TONY BRADMAN
illustrated by SARAH WARBURTON

STONE ARCH BOOKS®
a capstone imprint

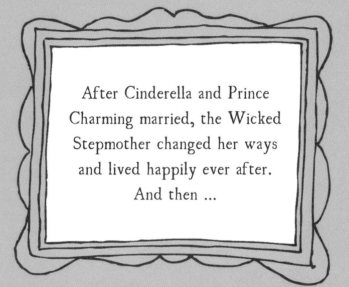

After Cinderella and Prince
Charming married, the Wicked
Stepmother changed her ways
and lived happily ever after.
And then ...

"There you go," said Cinderella, stepping back to admire her handiwork with a smile. "A change of hairdo, some funky clothes, and it's a totally new you!"

The Wicked Stepmother examined herself in the mirror, and she had to agree. Cinderella had done a great job of styling her from head to toe.

Cinderella was married to Prince Charming, but she had also started her own fashion business, Cinderella Makeovers Limited, and it was a huge success.

9

"Thanks, Cinderella," said the Wicked Stepmother. "You're so good to me, and I really don't deserve it. I can't believe how horrible I used to be to you!"

"Oh, stop it!" said Cinderella, giving her a hug.

"All I've done is improve the way you look on the outside. But you're a different person on the inside, too. You should be proud of yourself. Not many people can change like that."

It was true, the Wicked Stepmother had changed rather dramatically. She had felt so guilty when the Prince had put the glass slipper on Cinderella's foot and the amazing truth had come out.

That's when she realized she had treated Cinderella very badly, and she swore to be different from then on.

Luckily, Cinderella had completely forgiven her. She had forgiven the Ugly Sisters, too, and these days they both worked for Cinderella.

She had given them free makeovers, so they weren't quite as ugly anymore. In fact, life for all of them seemed much better. Although now there was a new problem.

"I'm glad I changed, honestly I am," said the Wicked Stepmother. "But at least being horrible used to keep me busy. Now I'm just so bored all the time!"

Tick tock

She let out a deep sigh. Every day was the same. She got up, got dressed, had breakfast, and sat around her cottage doing nothing. She'd certainly had enough daytime TV.

"I'm sorry to hear that," said Cinderella. "So what would you like to do?"

"I'd like to help people," said the Wicked Stepmother. "That way I could make up for all the bad stuff I did. I don't know how to go about it, though."

"What a wonderful idea!" said Cinderella. "It sounds to me as if you need some advice, and I happen to know exactly the right person to give it to you."

Cinderella made a quick phone call, then gave the Wicked Stepmother an address.

The address took her to the palace where Princess Daisy and Prince Freddy lived. Prince Freddy had been turned into a frog by a witch. But now he was human again, and he and his wife ran all the charities in the Forest.

"As you can see, helping people is definitely what we're all about here," said Princess Daisy. She gave the Wicked Stepmother a tour of their large office, which seemed very busy.

"There's a huge range of things you could get involved in. Although maybe you should start with something simple."

"And what could be simpler than going collecting donations for us?" said Prince Freddy with a big grin. "We always need money to help people."

Later that morning, the Wicked Stepmother found herself standing at the crossroads in the Forest. She was wearing a bright orange vest with the name of the charity she was collecting for, The Ugly Duckling Trust, written on it. She also had a cup to collect donations.

23

It was a cold day, and there weren't
many people out. A couple of young trolls
ran by and stuck their tongues out at her.

Mr. Wolf trotted past and said he was sorry, but he didn't have any money to spare.

And then a nasty old king rode up and
ordered her to get out of his way because
she was blocking the road!

The Wicked Stepmother very nearly lost
her temper with him, and then it started
to rain.

She trudged back through the Forest to
report back to Daisy and Freddy.

"Let's see, that's one fake coin, three buttons, and an acorn," said Daisy. "Oh dear, that didn't go too well. How about trying something else?"

"C-c-could it be indoors?" murmured the Wicked Stepmother, shivering.

"I've got just the thing," said Prince
Freddy with a smile. "Come with me."

He took her to a small, dusty room with a single desk in it. On the desk stood a great tottering tower of unopened letters, and a phone that was ringing.

Prince Freddy explained that the letters had been sent by people asking for help, and that he and Daisy needed someone to read them all.

"I think I can manage that," said the Wicked Stepmother as she sat down.

"It would be great if you could answer the phone too," said Freddy.

The next couple of hours were tough for the Wicked Stepmother. She started reading the letters, and soon she was engrossed in the sad stories.

Then the phone started ringing, and the stories she heard were even sadder than the ones she had read!

By the time she spoke to an old woman who lived in a shoe and had so many children she just didn't know what to do, the Wicked Stepmother was in tears.

"Ah, this doesn't seem to be going well either," said Daisy, handing the Wicked Stepmother a tissue. "Not to worry, there must be something for you."

But there wasn't. That night the Wicked Stepmother went home to her empty, little cottage. If she couldn't work for a charity, what could she do? She was beginning to think she would never help anyone.

The next morning the Wicked Stepmother
went to see Cinderella. But just as she was
going into Cinderella's store, she bumped into
someone she recognized.

"You're the Terrible Ogre, right?" she said.
"What are you doing here?"

"I've come for a makeover," said the Terrible Ogre miserably. "Although to be honest, it's not what I look like that needs to change, it's my personality."

"Really? Tell me about it," said the Wicked Stepmother with a smile. "There was a time not that long ago when I felt the same way."

So the Wicked Stepmother and the
Terrible Ogre sat and talked over a nice
cup of tea.

It turned out the Terrible Ogre was fed up with himself. He had made a lot of people unhappy. He wanted to change, but he didn't know how.

The Wicked Stepmother listened and
made some suggestions.

"Thank you so much!" the Terrible Ogre
said. "You're the first person I've met who
has made me feel that I really can change
if I want to."

"No problem," said the Wicked
Stepmother. "I was only trying to help."

"You've helped me a lot," said the Terrible Ogre. "Hey, I bet you could help others like me, too. You should do this kind of thing for a living. Goodbye!"

"Oh right, bye!" said the Wicked Stepmother.

"Helping others like him," she murmured. And then she grinned. "What a truly great idea!"

The one thing she knew about was how to change from being bad to being good. And there were plenty of characters in the Forest who needed to do just that.

She talked it over with Cinderella, who gave her some terrific advice about setting up a business.

A couple of weeks later, the Wicked Stepmother opened the Fairy Tale Clinic for Recovering Villains. Her first client was the Terrible Ogre, but she soon had many more.

She treated witches and giants and even
some other stepmothers. She spent every
day helping people, and they were all very
grateful.

The Wicked Stepmother was just happy to be busy, especially in a good way.

And so, strangely enough, the Wicked Stepmother and every villain in the Forest who walked through the doors of her clinic managed to live HAPPILY EVER AFTER!

ABOUT THE AUTHOR

Tony Bradman writes for children of all ages. He is particularly well known for his top-selling Dilly the Dinosaur series. His other titles include the Happily Ever After series, *The Orchard Book of Heroes and Villains*, and *The Orchard Book of Swords, Sorcerers,* and *Superheroes*. Tony lives in South East London.

ABOUT THE ILLUSTRATOR

Sarah Warburton is a rising star in children's books. She is the illustrator of the Rumblewick series, which has been very well received at an international level. The series spans across both picture books and fiction. She has also illustrated nonfiction titles and the Happily Ever After series. She lives in Bristol, England, with her young baby and husband.

GLOSSARY

admire (ad-MIRE) — to look at something and enjoy it

advice (ad-VICE) — a suggestion about what someone should do

charities (CHA-ruh-tees) — groups that raise money to help people in need

donations (DOH-nate-shuns) — things given without charge

engrossed (en-GROHST) — give something all your attention

examined (eg-ZAM-uhnd) — looked carefully at something

murmured (MUR-murd) — talked quietly

personality (pur-suh-NAL-uh-tee) — qualities or traits that make one person different from another

trudged (TRUHJT) — walked slowly and with effort

DISCUSSION QUESTIONS

1. Were you surprised that the Wicked Stepmother changed her ways? Why?

2. Cinderella forgave her stepmother and her stepsisters. Why is forgiveness important?

3. If you could start any charity, what would it be and why?

WRITING PROMPTS

1. Write a newspaper article about the Wicked Stepmother's new clinic.

2. Pick a favorite fairy-tale villian and write about how they changed after visiting the Wicked Stepmother.

3. The Wicked Stepmother wanted to help people. Write about a time when you helped someone.

THE FUN DOESN'T STOP HERE!

DISCOVER MORE AT...
WWW.CAPSTONEKIDS.COM

Find cool websites and more books like this
one at www.facthound.com.
Just type in the Book ID:
9781434279514